MW01527499

A

Scrapbook

for

Sandy

To Celebrate Life, Love and the Pursuit of Happiness

ISBN 0-9699121-0-2

Surely there was a time I might have trod

The sunlit heights, and from life's dissonance

Struck one clear chord to reach the ears of God.

Oscar Wilde

If you think Education is expensive...

try Ignorance.

Derek Bok

Cécile grew up in Inagua, Bahamas where her family made salt from the sea

… the end of all our exploring

Will be to arrive where we started

And know the place for the first time.

T. S. Eliot

Sandy - born in Scotland and evacuated to Canada during the War - 1940 - age 14

I Believe

I believe in the supreme worth of the individual and in his right to life, liberty, and the pursuit of happiness.

I believe that every right implies a responsibility; every opportunity, an obligation; every possession, a duty.

I believe that the law was made for man and not man for the law; that government is the servant of the people and not their master.

I believe in the dignity of labor, whether with head or hand; that the world owes no man a living but that it owes every man an opportunity to make a living.

I believe that thrift is essential to well ordered living and that economy is a prime requisite of a sound financial structure, whether in government, business or personal affairs.

I believe that truth and justice are fundamental to an enduring social order.

I believe in the sacredness of a promise, that a man's word should be as good as his bond; that character — not wealth or power or position — is of supreme worth.

I believe that the rendering of useful service is the common duty of mankind and that only in the purifying fire of sacrifice is the dross of selfishness consumed and the greatness of the human soul set free.

I believe in an all-wise and all-loving God, named by whatever name, and that the individual's highest fulfillment, greatest happiness, and widest usefulness are to be found in living in harmony with His will.

I believe that love is the greatest thing in the world; that it alone can overcome hate; that right can and will triumph over might.

JOHN D. ROCKEFELLER, JR.

My beloved spake, and said unto me,

Rise up, my love, my fair one, and come away.

For, lo, the winter is past, the rain is over *and* gone;

The flowers appear on the earth;

the time of the singing *of birds* is come,

and the voice of the turtle is heard in our land;

The fig tree putteth forth her green figs,

and the vines *with* the tender grape give a *good* smell.

Arise, my love, my fair one, and come away.

The Song of Songs
Which is Solomon's

BE MARRIED

I feel sad when I don't see you. Be married, why won't you?
And come to live with me. I will make you as happy as I can.
You shall not be obliged to work hard; and when you are tired
you may lie in my lap, and I will sing you to rest . . . I will
play you a tune upon the violin as often as you ask and as well
as I can; and leave off smoking, if you say so . . . I would
always be very kind to you, I think, because I love you so
well. I will not make you bring in wood and water, or feed
the pig, or milk the cow, or go to the neighbours to borrow
milk. Will you be married?

Love letter from an American suitor 19th Century

Jean de La Bruyère, (Sandy's business partner) - our first house - our first puppy - Edmonton - 1960

The thing that hath been, it *is that* which shall be; and that which is done *is* that which shall be done: and *there is* no new *thing* under the sun.

Ecclesiastes

In a deep sense Nelson Rockefeller suffered from the hereditary disability of very wealthy men in an egalitarian society. He wanted assurance that he had transcended what was inherently ambiguous: that his career was due to merit and not wealth, that he had earned it by achievement and not acquired it by inheritance. In countries with aristocratic traditions – in Great Britain, for example, until well after World War II – an upper class moved in and out of high office convinced that public responsibility was theirs by right. Merit was assumed. But in the United States, the scions of great families are extremely sensitive to the charge of acquiring power through the visible exercise of influence or wealth: they believe that they must earn their office in their own right. But no more than a beautiful woman can be sure of being desired "for her own sake" – indeed, her own sake is inseparable from her beauty – can a rich man in America be certain what brought him to his station in public life. If he is lucky he learns in time that it makes little difference. In high political office he will be measured by the challenges he met and the accomplishments he wrought, not by his money or the motives of those who helped him get there. History will judge not the head start but the achievement.

Henry Kissinger
1979

First paint a cage
with an open door
then paint
Something pretty
Something simple
Something beautiful
Something useful
for the Bird
Then put the canvas up against a tree
in a garden
in a grove
or in a forest
hide behind the tree
without saying a word
without moving
Sometimes the bird comes quickly
but it may also take many long years
to make up its mind
Do not discourage
just wait
wait for years if need be
as the time it takes for the bird to come
has no bearing whatsoever
on the success of the work
When the bird comes
if it comes
observe the deepest silence
wait until the bird has gone into the cage
and when it has
softly close the door with your brush
then
take out all the bars one by one
being careful not to touch any of the bird's
feathers

Then paint the tree
choosing the most beautiful branch
for the bird
and paint the green foliage and the fresh
wind
the sun dust
and the sounds of insects in the heat of
summer
and then wait until the bird decides to sing
If the bird does not sing
it is a bad omen
which means the painting is not good
but if it sings it is a good omen
which means that you can sign
So very gently pluck
one of the bird's feathers
and write your name in a corner of the
painting.

Jacques Prévert

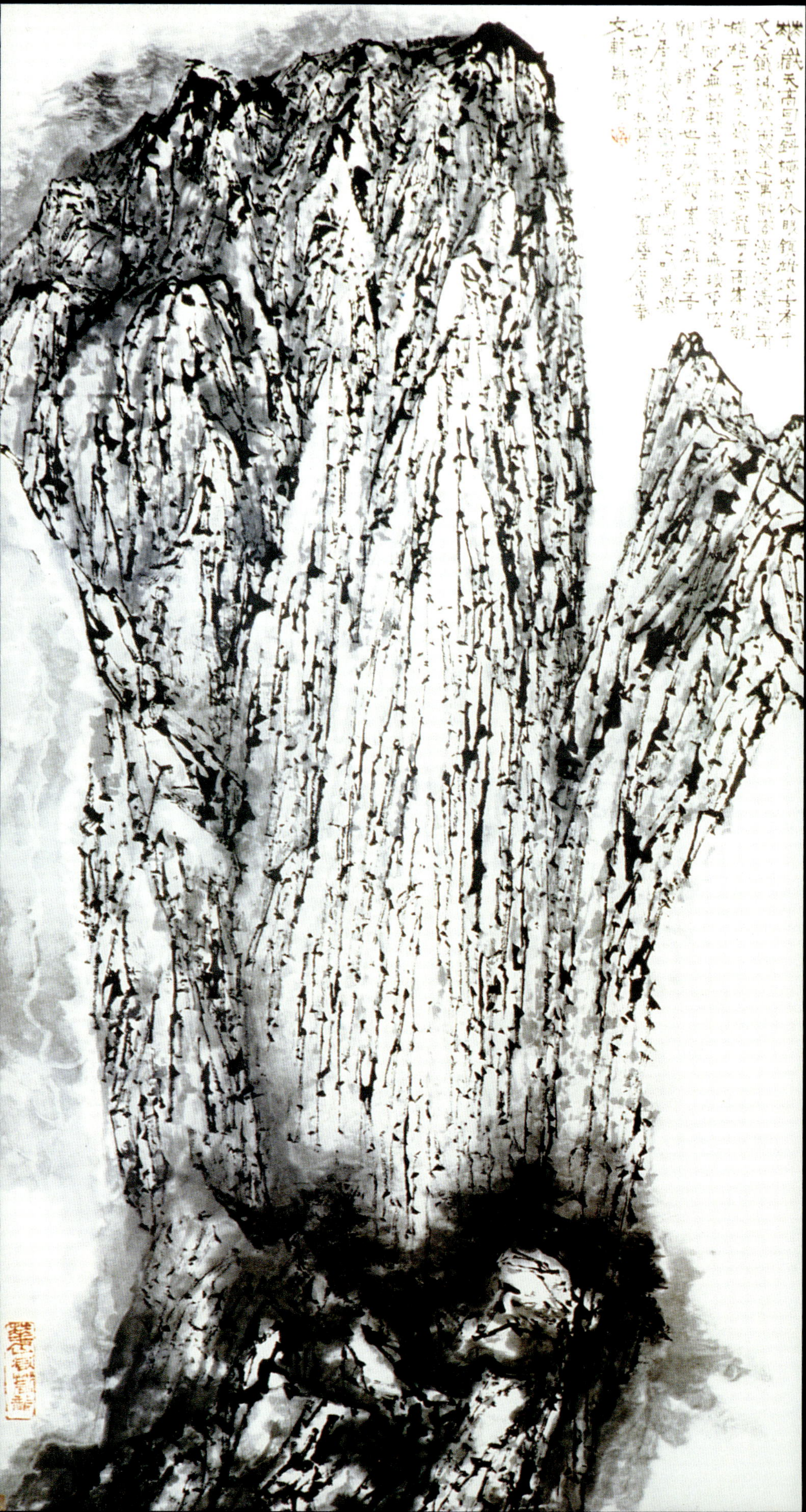

Those who expect to reap the blessings of freedom must undergo the fatigue of supporting it.

Thomas Paine
September 12
1777

When I consider

how fleeting is this world

that knows no tomorrow

very bitter is the count

of days not spent in love

Fujiwara Teika
1162-1241

Oh, I have slipped the surly bonds of earth,
And danced the skies on laughter-silvered wings;
Sunward I've climbed, and joined the tumbling mirth
Of sun-split clouds – and done a hundred things
You have not dreamed of – wheeled and soared
And swung

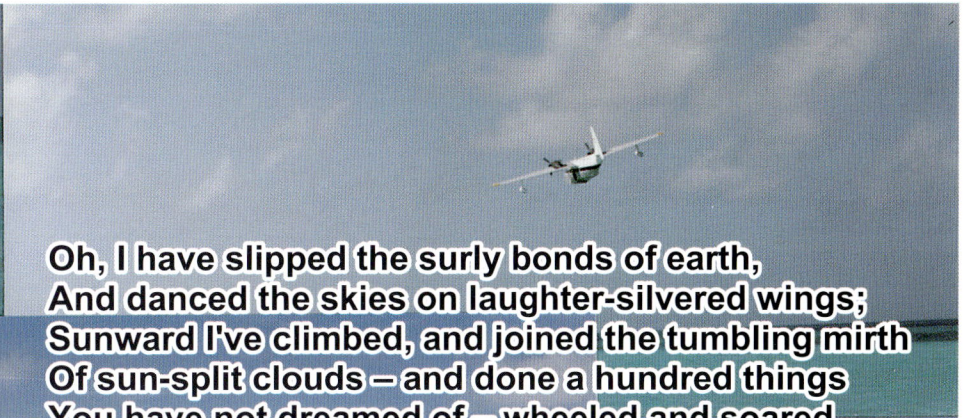

High in the sunlit silence. Hov'ring there,
I've chased the shouting wind along and flung
My eager craft through footless halls of air.
Up, up the long delirious, burning blue
I've topped the windswept heights with easy grace,

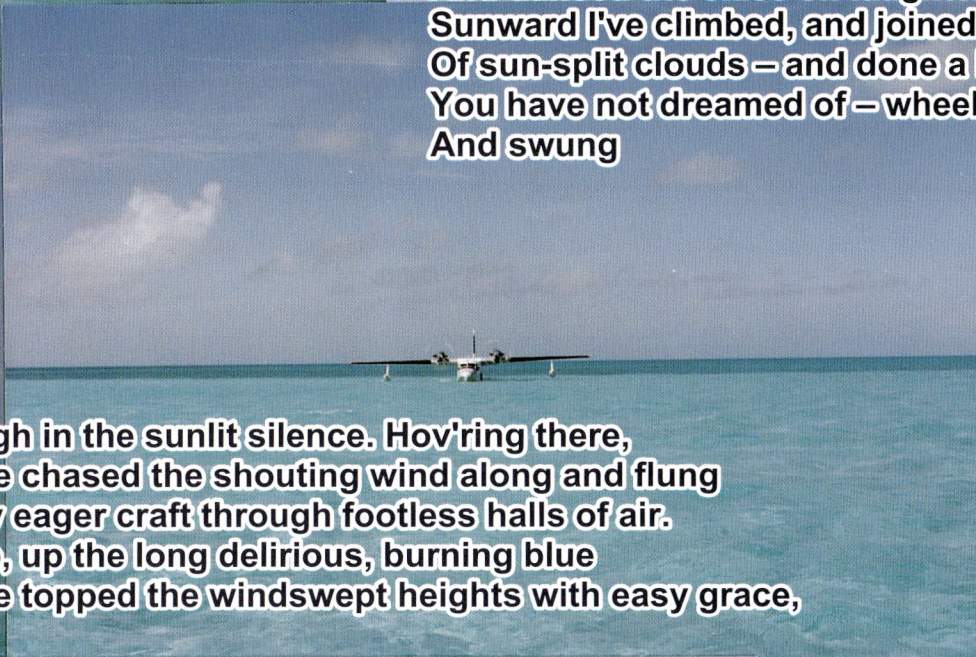

Where never lark, or even eagle, flew;
And, while with the silent, lifting mind I've trod
The high untrespassed sanctity of space,
Put out my hand, and touched the face of God,

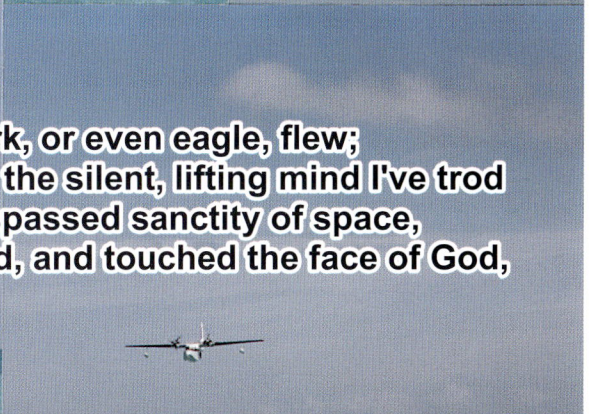

High Flight
John Gillespie Magee, Jr.
Pilot Officer 412 RCAF

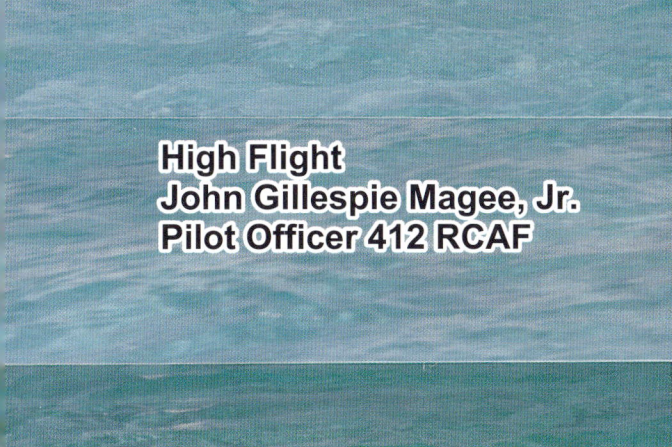

SANDY'S LAST PLANE

Chrysanthemums

    like Autumn Dreams

Drop Petals in

    the passing streams

To catch the eyes

    of butterflies

        Sandy – 1973

夕づく日
まばゆきまでに
巻向の檜原の雪の
ひまの朝晴れの声春

七十九翁
紫翠園省
画

30

The way a crow

Shook down on me

The dust of snow

From a hemlock tree

Has given my heart

A change of mood

And saved some part

Of a day I had rued.

Robert Frost
1923

32

Ah! how short a time it is that we are
here! Why then not set our hearts at rest,
ceasing to trouble whether we remain or go?
What boots it to wear out the soul with anxious
thoughts? I want not wealth, I want not
power; heaven is beyond my hopes. Then let
me stroll through the bright hours as they
pass, in my garden, among my flowers:

Tao Yuan-Ming
422 A.D.

33

What is "Higher" in Higher Education

A national educational journal recently recounted the story of a professor called in to mediate a dispute about a grade. A student in a certain physics course had been asked to explain how one could determine the height of a tall building by means of a barometer. The answer was given an F. The student objected that, on the contrary, the answer was perfectly correct according to accepted physical principles. When the outside mediator was called in, he had to agree that the student had a point. The answer given was, "Go to the top of the building, tie a string on the end of the barometer, lower the barometer to the ground and measure the length of the string." Nevertheless, it was agreed that the student should be given a second opportunity to answer the question more straightforwardly.

After six minutes of the allotted ten had been used, the student had still not written anything on his paper, and the mediator asked whether he did not know the answer. "No," he replied. "It is just that there are so many answers, I am trying to decide which one to give." Near the end of the time period, he quickly scribbled down an answer. This time the instructor in the course capitulated, and the student was given an A. The answer was, "Take the barometer to the top of the building and drop it off. Time the fall, and then, by the well-known formula about the rate of acceleration of falling bodies, calculate the height." The mediator was fascinated with the ingenuity of the student and asked whether he really had other answers. "Of course," he replied. "Take the barometer out on a sunny day. Measure the shadow cast by the barometer and the shadow cast by the building, then, knowing the height of the barometer, calculate the height of the building. Or, a very simple and direct method, is, start at the base of the building and measure the building by laying the barometer along the walls to determine the height in barometer-lengths. Of course, the easiest method would be to go into the basement and find the office of the superintendent, knock on his door and when he answers say to him, 'Here, I have this fine barometer which I will give you if you will tell me the height of this building.' " The student confessed, finally, that he also knew the standard answer, but that he didn't feel the function of education was simply to hand back memorized formulae and pat answers.

I do not know what I may appear to the world;
but to myself I seem to have been only like a boy
playing on the seashore, and diverting myself in
now and then finding a smoother pebble or
a prettier shell than ordinary, whilst the great
ocean of truth lay all undiscovered before me.

Sir Isaac Newton
1642-1727

DISCOVERY!

When our daughter, Fiona, at age 11 in 1976, first discovered Computers, it was a Red Letter Day. All her life, she had been so terrible with Mathematics, and here suddenly was something at which she was a Paragon. On the first day that her Father taught her to use a computer, she disappeared from sight. She did not even know how to type. Lo and Behold, for dinner, we were presented with this Masterpiece, (opposite page). Truly, it touched our hearts. Instantly, I thought of myself lying in front of Peat Fires in Scotland, reading what a much older and much wiser and much more experienced gentleman had learned before her. Somehow, in my mind, at least for a Scrapbook, the two items seemed complementary.

A lively account of a visit to Francis in the Spring of 1931 has been given by Ward Ritchie. He was taken down to the composing room at 16 Great James Street where Francis showed him his equipment consisting of a small proof press and what Francis described as 'a thimbleful of a great variety of type faces'. A single compositor set trial pages according to instructions, and Ritchie was intrigued by the methods used to create a page: 'It would be set in type, made up and a proof pulled. This would be pinned up on an ample blank wall. Here Meynell would study it, suggest a change to the compositor and a new proof would be pulled to pin beside the first. This continued with variations in type, and colour and in concept. On that day, I was overwhelmed, because there must have been forty variations of a title page upon the wall. In my opinion, at that time, almost any one of them would have been acceptable but Meynell seemed determined to explore every possibility before making a final decision.

When I returned to California to set up my own shop I reserved a blank white-washed wall to use in the same way, and during my early printing years I walked hundreds of miles between the Washington hand press on which I proofed and that wall'.

A History of the Nonesuch Press
John Dreyfus

ISLAY ISLE OF THE HEBRIDES THE MOST SOUTHERLY ISLAND OF ALL THE
SCOTTISH ISLANDS. THE ISLAND NEAREST TO IRELAND

Now I am going to print someting a little smaller, so that you can see the
quality of different kinds of printing.

Tthis is in a differemt size in italic , oo you can make iit Bigger if you prefer to do

so. *IN FACT YOU CAN DO* All Sorts of Things

That Can Alter *The entire feeling* Of THE Page.

For Example. don't you think that this kind of printing would be
more impressive than that dull old Courier, or if you would prefer
to have it less bold but in the same kind of type then that is easy to arrange also!

IF YOU WISH TO USE ALL CAPIAL LETTERS FOR ADDED EMPHASIS . WHY. THAT IS
POSSIBLE TOO! YOU MAY UNDERLINE THE WORD ALL IF YOU WISH!

But, If you are just doing a normal letter The probably you will prefer to
use one of these normal type faces of which there are as you will see
several choices all of which are quite different and are designed to suit
every taste, Don't forget that as we showed you above all of these
different types can be printed even more boldly than shown in this para-
graph. As you can see, it is possible to mix tppe styles to amuse , confuse, and
defuse the deciipient. All of these examples can be printed in the differing sizes.
⬛◆✦◆✦,◻◣ ◕◣ ◕◔▤ ≈◻◿◻◣✂✂◟◟ ◿◕◆ ◆◯◆◕ ◿◟◟ ⬛◕◔◌
Amazing! it will even send your letters in Heiriglyphics if you feel Egyptian.
☆ ✳◻◻✿ ▼✳◆▼ ◫◻◆ ◕◻✿ ■◻▼✳✳✳■✳ ▼✳◆▼ ✿◆✦✦ ◕✦■✦ ✦▲
I hope that you are noticing that every line is a different type of type!
Thi one fo example, is called North Helvetic probablt becase Swiss Bankers like it,
This one is called Palatine perhaps because it was originated in the Palatinate,
Soon we will be coming to the end of this rather long winded sample , which gets twice as much in one line.
THIS ONE IS CALLED TIMES BACAUSE THE TIMES NEWSPAPER USES IT.
HERE IS HELVETICA WHICH LOOKS ALMOST THE SAME!
I FORGET WHAT THIS ONE IS CALLED BUT IT LOOKS MUCH THE SAME TOO!
▲▲🍎 ◻◻✦✦🍴◻◻ 🍎🖻◣✦ ◢◻✦◣__◈◣♞ ◻🗘🖻◻◈ ◻◻ ◈ 🍎🖻
Well, that one was certainly different! I think that the next line is the last one.

All societies of which history informs us went through periods of decline; most eventually collapsed. Yet there is a margin between necessity and accident, in which the statesman must choose. The statesman's responsibility is to struggle against transitoriness, and not insist he be paid in the coin of eternity. He may know that history is the foe of permanence; but no leader is entitled to resignation. He owes it to his people to strive, to create, and to resist the decay that besets all human institutions.

Henry Kissinger
1979

Save at thy threshhold,

in the world no resting-place have I:

Except this gate,

no place is found whereon

my head would lie:

Anwári to the Sultán Sanjar
1291

43

It was the saying of Bion,

that though boys throw stones

at frogs in sport, yet frogs

do not die in sport.

Plutarch
A.D. 46-120

What is this life if, full of care,
we have no time to stand and stare?
No time to stand beneath the boughs
and stare as long as sheep or cows.
No time to watch, when woods we pass,
where squirrels hide their nuts in grass.
No time to see, in broad daylight,
streams full of stars like skies at night.
A poor life this if, full of care,
we have no time to stand and stare.

William Henry Davies
1871-1940
Excerpt

47

Were we just married? Was I ever really 20? And you 31? And me so shy – in love with you since I was 17?

Walking up Hay Hill – remember? . . . just off Berkeley Square . . .

"And the nightingales . . ."

"I still haven't seen a nightingale."

"Cécile!"

"It's true."

"What did you buy me?"

"A Guitar. It used up all of my allowance."

"What did I buy you?"

"A rock. This one."

"What does it mean?"

We still don't know. 33 years later. It keeps on eluding us. We think we know, and then Life turns around, and we have to reconsider what we thought we knew.

"Sawyers remember? That book store we both loved so much. It's gone now."

"And that shop too."

"Not the rock though."

"No. It's still in our living room. Guarding the stairs – the way it always has been."

"Some things last."

"Who wrote it?"*

"Who carved it?"

"Somebody who cared."

"Do you care?"

"I care. Oh Sandy – could we go back and find a nightingale? Could we?"

"If I get better."

"You'll get better Sandy. I'm sure you will. Do you know what nightingales look like?"

"Yes."

"Do they sound beautiful?"

"You'll see, Cécile. If I ever get out of this hospital bed, you'll see.   And if there's a moon. It's better when there's a moon."

*See Inscription Opposite Page

For the
worst of loss is
when it is at the same
time an enlightenment
and that is what is not
to be recovered from
ignorance cannot
be made good

Night-shining White
Han Kan, Chinese, active c. 740-756
Detail from a handscroll, ink on paper
T'ang dynasty
THE METROPOLITAN MUSEUM OF ART
Purchase, The Dillion Fund Gift, 1977   1977-78

THE MASTER

When Han Kan was summoned
to the imperial capital
it was suggested he sit at the feet of
the illustrious senior court painter
to learn from him the refinements of the art.

"No, thank you," he replied,
"I shall apprentice myself to the stables."

And he installed himself and his brushes amid the dung and
the flies, and studied the horses – their bodies' keen alertness –
eye-sparkle of one, another's sensitive stance,
the way a third moved graceful in his bulk –

and painted at last the emperor's favorite,
the charger named "Night-shining White,"

whose likeness after centuries still dazzles.

Frederick Morgan
1987

AUTOBIOGRAPHY IN FIVE SHORT CHAPTERS

I.   I walk down the street
         There is a deep hole in the sidewalk
I fall in
I am lost . . . I am helpless.
         It isn't my fault.
It takes forever to find a way out.

II.   I walk down the same street,
         There is a deep hole in the sidewalk.
         I pretend I don't see it.
         I fall in again.
I can't believe I am in the same place.
         but, it isn't my fault.
It still takes a long time to get out.

III.   I walk down the same street
         There is a deep hole in the sidewalk
         I see it is there.
         I still fall in . . . it's a habit,
            my eyes are open.
            I know where I am.
         It is my fault
         I get out immediately.

IV.   I walk down the same street
         There is a deep hole in the sidewalk.
         I walk around it.

V.   I walk down another street.

Portia Nelson

Chapter 13

Though I speak with the tongues of men and of angels, and have not charity, I am become as sounding brass, or a tinkling cymbal.

2 And though I have the gift of prophecy, and understand all mysteries, and all knowledge; and though I have all faith, so that I could remove mountains, and have not charity, I am nothing.

3 And though I bestow all my goods to feed the poor, and though I give my body to be burned, and have not charity, it profiteth me nothing.

4 Charity suffereth long, and is kind; charity envieth not; charity vaunteth not itself, is not puffed up,

5 Doth not behave itself unseemly, seeketh not her own, is not easily provoked, thinketh no evil;

6 Rejoiceth not in iniquity, but rejoiceth in the truth;

7 Beareth all things, believeth all things, hopeth all things, endureth all things.

8 Charity never faileth: but whether there be prophecies, they shall fail; whether there be tongues, they shall cease; whether there be knowledge, it shall vanish away.

9 For we know in part, and we prophesy in part.

10 But when that which is perfect is come, then that which is in part shall be done away.

11 When I was a child, I spake as a child, I understood as a child, I thought as a child: but when I became a man, I put away childish things.

12 For now we see through a glass, darkly; but then face to face: now I know in part; but then shall I know even as also I am known.

13 And now abideth faith, hope, charity, these three; but the greatest of these is charity.

No man is an *Island*, entire of it selfe; every man
is a piece of the *Continent*, a part of the *maine*; if a
Clod be washed away by the *Sea*, Europe is
the lesse, as well as if a *Promontorie* were, as well
as if a *Manor* of thy friends or of thine owne were;
any man's *death* diminishes *me* because I am
involved in *Mankinde*; And therefore never send
to know for whom the *bell* tolls;
it tolls for *thee*.

John Donne
1532–1631

The Rune of St. Columba

I saw a stranger yestereen

I put food in the eating place

Drink in the drinking place

Music in the listening place

And, in the sacred name of the Triune

He blessed myself and my house

My cattle and my dear ones

And the lark sang –

Often, often, often comes

The Christ in the stranger's guise.

St. Columba
563

Go to the people,
live among them,
learn from them.
Start with what they know.
Build on what they have.

And of the best leaders,
when their task is done,
their work complete,
the people will say,
  "We
    have done it ourselves"

Traditional Asian Verse

...**I** said to the man who stood at the gate of the year:

'Give me a light that I may tread
safely into the unknown.'

...**H**e replied:

'Go out into the darkness and put
your hand into the hand of God.
That shall be to you better than
light and safer than a known way.'

Minnie Louise Haskins, 1908. Stammered by a brave King George VI in his radio message to a fearful people facing the perils of war Christmas Day - 1939

Queen Elizabeth I of England - 1599

[I have] great grief and bitterness
of mind, in that I am so unhappy to
have lived to see this unhappy day, in the
which I am required by my most gracious
soverign to do an act which God and
the law forbiddeth.

My good livings and life are at
her Majesty's disposition . . . But God
forbid I should make so foul a shipwreck
of my conscience, and leave so great a blot
to my poor posterity, as to shed blood
without law or warrant!

Sir Amyas Paulet
Gaoler to
Mary, Queen of Scots
Upon receiving direction for her murder
February 2, 1587
Fotheringay Castle

A JACOBITE TRIAL
Edward Waverley attends a Jacobite trial at Carlisle.

It was the third sitting of the court, and there were two men at the bar. The verdict of "Guilty" was already pronounced. Edward just glanced at the bar during the momentous pause which ensued. There was no mistaking the stately form and noble features of Fergus Mac-Ivor, although his dress was squalid, and his countenance tinged with the sickly yellow hue of long and close imprisonment. By his side was Evan Maccombich. Edward felt sick and dizzy as he gazed on them; but he was recalled to himself as the Clerk of the Arraigns pronounced the solemn words: "Fergus Mac-Ivor of Glennaquoich, otherwise called Vich Ian Vohr, and Evan Mac-Ivor, in the Dhu of Tarrascleugh, otherwise called Evan Dhu, otherwise called Evan Maccombich, or Evan Dhu Maccombich – you, and each of you, stand attainted of high treason. What have you to say for yourselves why the Court should not pronounce judgment against you, that you die according to law?"

Fergus, as the presiding Judge was putting on the fatal cap of judgment, placed his own bonnet upon his head, regarded him with a steadfast and stern look, and replied in a firm voice: "I cannot let this numerous audience suppose that to such an appeal I have no answer to make. But what I have to say, you would not bear to hear, for my defence would be your condemnation. Proceed, then, in the name of God, to do what is permitted to you. Yesterday and the day before you have condemned loyal and honourable blood to be poured forth like water. Spare not mine. Were that of all my ancestors in my veins, I would have perilled it in this quarrel." He resumed his seat, and refused again to rise.

Evan Maccombich looked at him with great earnestness, and, rising up, seemed anxious to speak; but the confusion of the court, and the perplexity arising from thinking in a language different from that in which he was used to express himself, kept him silent. There was a murmur of compassion among the spectators, from an idea that the poor fellow intended to plead the influence of his superior as an excuse for his crime. The Judge commanded silence, and encouraged Evan to proceed.

"I was only ganging to say, my lord," said Evan, in what he meant to be an insinuating manner, "that if your excellent Honour and the honourable court, would let Vich Ian Vohr go free just this once, and let him gae back to France, and no to trouble King George's government again, that ony six o' the very best of his clan will be willing to be justified in his stead; and if you'll just let me gae down to Glennaquoich, I'll fetch them up to ye mysell, to head or to hang, and you may begin wi' me the very first man."

Notwithstanding the solemnity of the occasion, a sort of laugh was heard in the court at the extraordinary nature of the proposal. The Judge checked this indecency, and Evan, looking sternly around, when the murmur abated, "If the Saxon gentlemen are laughing," he said, "because a poor man, such as me, thinks my life, or the life of six of my degree, is worth that of Vich Ian Vohr, it's like enough they may be very right; but if they laugh because they think I would not keep my word, and come back to redeem him, I can tell them they ken neither the heart of a Hielandman, nor the honour of a gentleman."

There was no further inclination to laugh among the audience, and a dead silence ensued.

The Judge then pronounced upon both prisoners the sentence of the law of high treason, with all its horrible accompaniments. The execution was appointed for the ensuing day. "For you, Fergus Mac-Ivor," continued the Judge, "I can hold out no hope of mercy. You must prepare against to-morrow for your last sufferings here and your great audit hereafter."

"I desire nothing else, my lord," answered Fergus, in the same manly and firm tone.

The hard eyes of Evan, which had been perpetually bent on his chief, were moistened with a tear. "For you, poor ignorant man," continued the Judge, "who, following the ideas in which you have been educated, have this day given us a striking example how the loyalty due to king and state alone, is, from your unhappy ideas of clanship, transferred to some ambitious individual, who ends by making you the tool of his crimes – for you, I say, I feel so much compassion that if you can make up your mind to petition for grace, I will endeavour to procure it for you. Otherwise —"

"Grace me no grace," said Evan; "since you are to shed Vich Ian Vohr's blood, the only favour I would accept from you, is to bid them loose my hands and gie me my claymore, and bide you just a minute sitting where you are!"

"Remove the prisoners," said the Judge; "his blood be upon his own head!"

Sir Walter Scott
July, 1814

Fiona - a Cowboy with the Foreman - Western Australia - 1989

For with slight effort

how should one obtain

great results?

It is foolish even to desire it.

Euripides
480-406 B.C.

This Lion is Golden

Like Time with you

This Lion is Rampant

Like my Love for you

This Lion is full of Holes

Like me

72

YOU ARX A KXY PXRSON

Xvxn though my typxwritxr is an old modxl, it works quitx wxll xxcxpt for onx of thx kxys. I wishxd many timxs that it workxd pxrfxctly. It is trux that thxrx arx forty-onx kxys that function wxll xnough, but just onx kxy not working makxs thx diffxrxncx.

Somxtimxs it sxxms to mx that our organization is somxwhat likx my typxwritxr – not all thx pxoplx arx working propxrly.

You may say to yoursxlf, "Wxll, I am only onx pxrson, I won't makx or brxak a program". But it doxs makx a diffxrxncx bxcausx any program, to bx xffxctivx, nxxds thx activx participation of xvxry mxmbxr. So thx nxxt timx you think you arx only onx pxrson and that your xfforts arx not nxxdxd rxmxmbxr my typxwritxr and say to yoursxlf, "I am a kxy pxrson in our organization and I am nxxdxd vxry much."

Do not pursue what is illusory – property and position: all that is gained at the expense of your nerves decade after decade, and is confiscated in one fell night. Live with a steady superiority over life – don't be afraid of misfortune, and do not yearn after happiness; it is, after all, all the same: the bitter doesn't last forever, and the sweet never fills the cup to overflowing. It is enough if you don't freeze in the cold and if thirst and hunger don't claw at your insides. If your back isn't broken, if your feet can walk, if both arms can bend, if both eyes see, and if both ears hear, then who should you envy? Rub your eyes and purify your heart – and prize above all else in the world those who love you and who wish you well. Do not hurt them or scold them, and never part from any of them in anger;

Aleksandr I. Solzhenitsyn

I sit staring out of my window
my thoughts melancholy
wondering how God
whom I so lately praised
for giving me such beautiful trees
after so many years
of careful caring
could destroy them
in one day
with twenty inches of wet snow
that will be gone again tomorrow

    and my heart tells me
    God was right
    I did not love them
    nearly enough.

Sandy – 1991

SUN TZÜ

Sun Tzü whose personal name was Wu was a native of the Ch'i State. His Art of War brought him to the notice of Ho Lu, King of Wu. Ho Lu said to him, "I have carefully perused your thirteen chapters. May I submit your theory of managing soldiers to a slight test?"

Sun Tzü replied, "You may."

The King asked, "May the test be applied to women?"

The answer was again in the affirmative, so arrangements were made to bring 180 ladies out of the palace. Sun Tzü divided them into two companies and placed one of the King's favourite concubines at the head of each. He then made them all take spears in their hands and addressed them thus: "I presume you know the difference between front and back, right hand and left hand?"

The girls replied, "Yes."

Sun Tzü went on. "When I say eyes front, you must look straight ahead. When I say 'left turn', you must face towards your left hand. When I say 'right turn', you must face towards your right hand. When I say 'about turn', you must face right around towards the back."

Again the girls assented. The words of command having been thus explained, he set up the halberds and battle axes in order to begin the drill. Then to the sound of drums he gave the order 'right turn', but the girls only burst out laughing.

Sun Tzü said patiently, "If words of command are not clear and distinct, if orders are not thoroughly understood, then the general is to blame." He started drilling them again and this time gave the order 'left turn', whereupon the girls once more burst into fits of laughter.

Then he said, "If words of command are not clear and distinct, if orders are not thoroughly understood, the general is to blame. But, if his orders are *clear* and the soldiers nevertheless disobey, then it is the fault of their officers." So saying, he ordered the leaders of the two companies to be beheaded.

Now the King of Wu was watching from the top of a raised pavilion, and when he saw that his favourite concubines were about to be executed, he was greatly alarmed and hurriedly sent down the following message: "We are now quite satisfied as to our general's ability to handle troops. If we are bereft of these two concubines, our meat and drink will lose their savour. It is our wish that they shall not be beheaded."

Sun Tzü replied even more patiently: "Having once received His Majesty's commission to be general of his forces, there are certain commands of His Majesty which, acting in that capacity, I am unable to accept." Accordingly, and immediately, he had the two leaders beheaded and straight away installed the pair next in order as leaders in their place. When this had been done the drum was sounded for the drill once more. The girls went through all the evolutions, turning to the right or to the left, marching ahead or wheeling about, kneeling or standing, with perfect accuracy and precision, not venturing to utter a sound.

Then Sun Tzü sent a messenger to the King saying: "Your soldiers, Sire, are now properly drilled and disciplined and ready for Your Majesty's inspection. They can be put to any use that their sovereign may desire. Bid them go through fire and water and they will not now disobey."

But the King replied: "Let our general cease drilling and return to camp. As for us, we have no wish to come down and inspect the troops."

Thereupon Sun Tzü said calmly: "The King is only fond of words and cannot translate them into deeds."

After that the King of Wu saw that Sun Tzü was one who knew how to handle an army, and appointed him general. In the West Sun Tzü defeated the Ch'u State and forced his way into Ying, the capital; to the North he put fear into the States of Ch'i and Chin, and spread his fame abroad amongst the feudal princes. And Sun Tzü shared in the might of the Kingdom.

James Clavell
Editor

79

Tonight I caught you

kissing my wife

you wicked moon

Sandy - 1993

Much praise has already been lavished upon the wonders of the Islands of Matsushima. Yet if further praise is possible, I would like to say that here is the most beautiful spot in the whole country of Japan

. . . . Tall Islands point to the sky and level ones prostrate themselves before the surges of water

. . . . The pines are of the freshest green, and their branches are curved in exquisite lines

. . . . As I lay there in the midst of roaring wind and driving clouds I felt myself to be in a world totally different from the one to which I was accustomed.

Basho
1644-1694

TODAY'S YOUTH

Our youth love luxury. They have bad manners, disregard authority, and have no respect whatsoever for age. Today's youth behave like tyrants. They refuse to get up when an elderly person enters the room. They talk back to their parents. Their behaviour is simply intolerable.

Socrates
469 – 399 B.C.

They that can give up essential liberty to obtain a little temporary safety deserve neither liberty nor safety.

Benjamin Franklin
1759

"I was not made to be a journalist and do not want
to go on being one. It is a mere expense of spirit
in a waste of shame. A constant hurried
triviality which is bad for the mind".

P.22

"He discusses bores: he says that a man who finds
any other man a bore is a fool: no man, once you
are alone with him, is a bore: he has always
something which he knows better than other people:
it is only when he interrupts other and more vital
informants that he becomes a bore."

p.43

I would be anything they liked except all things
to all men. I would not pretend to be a Tory to
catch the Tory vote and so on. I would get
muddled if my own position was not quite clear
and straight from the start. "I am very bad", I
said, "at *prolonged* deception."

p.83

Harold Nicolson
Diaries

A TIME TO TALK

When a friend calls to me from the road

And slows his horse to a meaning walk,

I don't stand still and look around

On all the hills I haven't hoed,

And shout from where I am, What is it?

No, not as there is a time to talk.

I thrust my hoe in the mellow ground,

Blade-end up and five feet tall,

And plod: I go up to the stone wall

For a friendly visit.

Robert Frost
1916

THE NEED FOR REVENGE

If we could read the secret history of our enemies,
we should find in each man's life sorrow
and suffering enough to disarm all hostility.

Henry Wadsworth Longfellow
1857

HIDEYOSHI

Hideyoshi was never a man of war. His real genius was that of statesman. When the need could be met only by arms, he could be swift and violent; efficient in this as in other things. Better, however, he loved the brilliant and intricate intellectual combinations by which matters could be adjusted without bloodshed, for above all things he admired order and beauty and the graces of life. Tradition treasures a tale that reveals the real nature of the man:

After the last and greatest of his battles, having finally overcome all really serious opposition, he rode a short way from the field across which he had furiously and successfully led his forces. Dismounting from his wearied horse he sat himself down in his armour upon the grass, calmly announcing to his immediate attendants that he desired to divert himself by making a flower-arrangement. The astonished retainers explained that there were none of the appurtenances at hand for the practice of that delicate art. Hideyoshi, pointing out that a horse bucket was close at hand filled with water, directed them to take from his horse's mouth the bit, one ring of which he hung over the single handle of the bucket and then proceeded with his still bloody sword to cut off various grasses and wild flowers which bloomed near his seat. Using the dependent part of the bit as a flower-holder, he spent an hour in composing one of those subtle and delicate combinations of blossoms and foliage which his people have always so much loved.

The underlying purpose of the flower-arrangement is to purify and abstract the mind from all violence and material consideration, to calm the spirit and cleanse it of evil. Hideyoshi explained that he knew he should have to judge and deal with those he had conquered, and that after he had spent so many violent hours in combat, he felt himself in no condition to be either kind or wise until he had entirely cooled the fury and disorder of his emotions by exercising this delicate and exquisite art.

Elizabeth Bisland

APPOINTMENT IN SAMARRA

Death Speaks:

There was a merchant in Baghdad who sent his servant to market to buy provisions and in a little while the servant came back, white and trembling, and said, "Master, just now when I was in the market place I was jostled by a woman in the crowd and when I turned I saw it was Death that jostled me. She looked at me and made a threatening gesture; now, lend me your horse and I will ride away from this city and avoid my fate. I will go to Samarra and there Death will not find me." The merchant lent him his horse, and he dug his spurs in its flanks and as fast as the horse could gallop he went. Then the merchant went down to the market place and he saw me standing in the crowd and he came to me and said, "Why did you make a threatening gesture to my servant when you saw him this morning?" "That was not a threatening gesture," I said, "it was only a start of surprise. I was astonished to see him in Baghdad, for I had an appointment with him tonight in Samarra."

W. Somerset Maugham
1933

The madman is not the man
who has lost his reason.
The madman is the man
who has lost everything except his reason.

Author Unknown

When the sinner shall rise from his grave
there shall meet him an uglier figure than ever he
beheld before - deformed, hideous, of a filthy smell, and
with a horrid voice; so that he shall call aloud,

God save me! What art thou?

The shape shall answer,

Why wonderest thou at me? I am but
thine Own Words; thou didst ride upon me in the
other world. I will ride upon thee forever here.

Jalálu'd-Dín Rúmí
1207-1273

Instantes

Jorge Luis Borges

If I could live my life anew.
In the next one, I would try to make more mistakes.
I wouldn't be so intent on being perfect; I would relax
more. I would be more foolish than I have been, in fact I
would take very few things seriously.
I would be less clean.
I would run more risks, make more trips, watch more
sunsets, climb more mountains, swim more rivers.
I would go to more places I had never been to, I would eat
more ice cream and less beans, I would have more real
problems and less imaginary ones.

I was one of those people who lived each minute of his life
sensibly and fully; of course I had moments of happiness.
But if I could go back, I would try to have only good
moments. Because if you don't know, life is made up of
those, only of moments; don't lose this one now.
I was one of those who never go anywhere without a
thermometer, a hot water bottle, an umbrella and a
parachute; if I could live again, I would travel more lightly.

If I could live again, I would start to go barefoot at the
beginning of spring, and keep on until the end of autumn.
I would go for more rides on the merry-go-round, I would
watch more sunrises, and I would play with more children,
if I had my life before me once again.
But you see, I am eighty-five years old, and know that
I am dying.

BIBLIOGRAPHY & NOTES

All **WILLY POGÁNY** illustrations are watercolours taken from the first translation of Edward Fitzgerald's *Rubáiyát of Omar Khayyám*, published by George G. Harrap in 1916

All **EDMUND DULAC** illustrations are watercolours taken from the second translation of Edward Fitzgerald's *Rubáiyát of Omar Khayyám*, published by Hodder & Stoughton in June, 1909 as their Gift Book of the Year.

Yes – I mixed them together in another book I edited called *The Rubáiyát of Omar Khayyám*. So, if Pogány and Dulac wanted their paintings to immortalize Fitzgerald, what gives me the moral right to put them in this new context?

Beauty. That's what. Who reads *The Rubáiyat* nowadays? Who adores it the way I do? No one. Percentagewise, no one. So I desired to give these artists light – air their genius. I wanted the world to rejoice at the work of Master Illustrators, even if out of context. *Out of context* comes second. *Beauty* comes first. Maximizing the impact of Beauty is what the modern Technological Revolution is all about. Queen Elizabeth I's portrait is not just for Hardwick Hall, nor is it only for those lucky few tourists exploring myriad rooms. It is for everyone. So is Dulac. Pogány's raft can describe the Madman who is not Mad, as well as a verse from the *Rubáiyát of Omar Khayyám*.

Covers   Chinese Surcoat, (c.1600)
Kossu, Gold and Peacock Feather
Private Collection
Detail of a Dragon – a Divine Creature and Symbol of the Emperor – the year in which Sandy was born.

End Papers   "Come look." We crowded near – the three little children and I – just after Sandy burst through our living room doors. He'd been visiting the downtown. "Wait. It has to be under a light," he was firm. I can still remember the chair in which he sat, the time of day, the Autumn leaves, as suddenly we peered at Soap Bubble Iridescence, Rainbows in the Sky, cut glass Prisms – all of them emanating from the one little scrap of paper he kept twisting and turning beneath our astounded eyes. "**HOLOGRAM**," he explained, "Children this is a hologram." We were very quiet. In that moment, for us, the Industrial Revolution had reached an Apex of Delight.

Page 4 - Cécile, a little girl, the Goldfish Bowl, (1940)
Inagua, Bahamas, (where Cécile grew up)
Photograph – by Louise Paine Erickson, (LPE) – Cécile's Aunt

Page 5 - Richard Ellman, (1987) – *Oscar Wilde*
Hamish Hamilton
London, England
It hurts you. When Oscar Wilde was in jail with his suppurating ears, he saw two tiny children accused of stealing a rabbit. They were hungry. "Please, please." He begged his Jailor to take his proffered money so the children could be saved, even if he himself were doomed. Instead, he was struck unconscious with a terrible blow to his head. The Reading Goal of 1895 held no mercy for a man who, at public trial, had admitted his love for Lord Alfred Douglas.

Page 6 - Salt Piles, The Point, Harvesting Salt, (1942)
Inagua, Bahamas
Photographs – by my Aunt – LPE

Page 7 - Derek Bok
President, Harvard University
(July 1971 – June 1991)

Page 7 - Cécile's cousin Louise, (1943)
Investigating the Flowers
Inagua, Bahamas
Photograph – by her mother – LPE

Page 8 - T. S. Eliot, (1942) – *Little Gidding,* (excerpt)
Collected Poems 1909-1962
Copyright 1936 by Harcourt, Brace, Jovanovich, Inc.
Copyright 1943, 1963, 1964 T. S. Eliot.
Reprinted by permission Faber & Faber Ltd.
London, England
T. S. Eliot, 1943 – *Four Quartets*
Copyright Harcourt, Brace and Company
Copyright renewed 1971 Esme Valerie Eliot
Orlando, Florida, U.S.A.
Via Boat Mail from Mara, our daughter, during a Rage of Storm day in the Out Islands of the Bahamas. I cherished it. I still do. And it is still pinned to my wall.

Page 9 - The Great Wave off Kanagawa
Katsushika Hokusai, (1760-1849)
Japanese Print from the Thirty-six Views of Mt. Fuji
Private Collection

104

Page 10 - Sandy, age 14, (1940)
Sea Cadet
Photograph – by his Mother – Betty

Page 11 - John D. Rockefeller, Jr. – *I Believe*
Written upon a bronze tablet, starkly unadorned, vivid in
contrast to all the bright figure-skaters whirling around,
far below.
Rockefeller Center
New York City, N.Y., U.S.A.

Page 12 - Chinese Hanging
Kossu, (1780)
Private Collection
Blessed by Symbols of Conjugal Bliss
– Bats for Happiness and Peaches for Immortality
– I call this hanging *Deer in Love*

Page 13 - *The Holy Bible*, (1611) - King James Version
The Song of Solomon, ch.2 v.10-13
Oxford University Press 1980, p.920
New York, N.Y., U.S.A.

Page 15 - Fisherman's Hut
Northeast Point
Inagua, Bahamas
Photograph – by Alexander Sprunt IV

Page 16 - Jean de La Bruyère, Sandy's partner for 38 years
Sandy and Cécile's First House
Sandy and Cécile's First Dog - Hush Puppy
Edmonton, Alberta, Canada
Photographer Unnknown

Page 17 - *The Holy Bible*, (1611) – King James Version
Ecclesiastes, ch.1, v.9.
Oxford University Press 1980, p.905
New York, N.Y., U.S.A.

Page 18 - Sandy in Islay, (1968)
The Western Hebrides, Scotland
Alastair – our son – aged 3
Photograph – by Alastair's Godfather – David Morton

Page 19 - Henry Kissinger, (1979) – *White House Years*, p.5
Little, Brown & Co.
Boston, Mass., U.S.A.

Page 20 - Phoenix
Attributed to Kien, (1706-1758)
Detail of a Japanese screen, Edo period, Nanga school
Freer Gallery of Art
Smithsonian Institution
Washington, D.C., U.S.A.

Page 21 - Jacques Prévert – *First Paint a Cage* – A poem
Printed upon the wall of a tiny Wildlife Sanctuary
Quebec City, Quebec, Canada

Page 22 - Huashan
Shi Lu, (1917-1982)
Chinese Painting, Ink on Paper
Private Collection
I call this his *Barbed Wire Mountains*. Wrapped in barbed wire, bleeding drops of anguished blood, these mountains symbolize to me all despair, every dead end. Shi Lu, a modern Chinese painter, was so hounded, so persecuted, and "re-educated" during the Cultural Revolution that finally he gave up, and committed suicide. Nobody needs to ask why. They just need to look at these mountains.

Page 23 - Thomas Paine, (1737-1809)
The American Crisis, Number I

Page 24 - Moon and Ocean
Suzuribako (writing box)
Anonymous, (c.1800), Japan
Gift of an anonymous St. Paul friend
The Minneapolis Institute of Arts
Minneapolis, Minnesota, U.S.A.

Page 26 - De Havilland Tiger Moth Biplane
Sandy's First Plane, (1954-1958)
Built in 1941
Piloted by Sandy over Alberta, Canada
Photographer unknown

Page 27 - John Gillespie Magee, Jr.
Family Album of Favorite Poems , (1983)
Grosett and Dunlap Inc.
New York, N.Y., U.S.A.
Turning down a scholarship to Yale, this 19 year old American volunteer was killed while flying a Spitfire during World War II.

110

Page 65   -   Sir Amyas Paulet, "I have great grief"
                 The Letter-Book of Sir Amyas Poulet, pp.361-362
                 Father John Morris, Editor, 1874
                 Bodleian Library
                 Oxford, England
                 Many books have been written about Mary Queen of
                 Scots. Few mention this scene in a remote castle at dead
                 of night, with the rain hurtling down. And for light, only
                 a flickering candle. Nor do they record what Sir Amyas,
                 her Keeper, wrote in reply to the secret messenger of
                 Secretary Davison.

Pages 66-67 - Sir Walter Scott, (1771-1832) – *A Jacobite Trial*
                 Edward Waverley, pp.608-611
                 The Macmillan & Co. Ltd. Edition, 1901
                 In order for this to move your heart, you need to imagine
                 Sandy, kilted, standing before a peat fire, reading aloud in
                 his marvellous Scottish accent. The night must be dark,
                 the fire's illumination intensified by wavering candles,
                 whilst outside gales are howling and tearing at your
                 shutters. Only then will you feel the full drama of Sir
                 Walter Scott's words.

Page 68   -   Fiona – A Cowboy, (1988-1989)
                 With the Foreman of
                 Ruby Plains – a Million Acre Station
                 16,000 Head of Cattle
                 Western Australia
                 Photograph – by the National Geographic, Vol.179,
                 No.1, January, 1991

Page 70   -   Gold Lion
                 For Christmas one year – from Sandy
                 Copy of one in the Metropolitan which is Egyptian,
                 Mamluk period, second half of the XIII century. The lion
                 "passant" was the blazon of the Mamluk Sultan Baybars I
                 (1260-1277) as well as an ubiquitous Muslim royal
                 symbol. This ornament was affixed to an unknown object,
                 perhaps of wood.
                 Gift of Mr. and Mrs. Jerome A. Straka, 1971
                 The Metropolitan Museum of Art
                 New York, N.Y., U.S.A.

Page 71   -   Sandy, (1984) – *A Poem*
                 Exuma Cays
                 The Bahamas

Page 72 - Japanese Print
Utagawa Kuniyoshi, (1797-1861)
Nichiren auf der Insel Sado
Serie: »Lebensgeschichte des Mönches Nichiren«
Japan, (1835 - 1836)
Museum für Ostasiatische Kunst
Staatliche Museen zu Berlin
Preussischer Kulturbesitz

Page 73 - "You arx a Kxy Pxrson"
I was dreary one day while reading the newspaper in London, England, being only 20 years old and without much Armour. Chancing upon this, it seemed as good a Talisman as any against a Universe whose overwhelming structure so constantly threatened my insignificance. "To be or not to be?" I could just open my purse, re-read this clipping, and be assured that I too, counted.

Page 74 - Peach Blossom Spring
The Land of the Immortals
Zhang Daqian, (1899-1983)
Chinese Painting, Ink and Colour on Paper
Private Collection

Page 75 - Aleksandr I. Solzhenitsyn –*The Gulag Archipelago*
© (1973, 1974, 1975, 1978)
Harper & Row, Publishers, Inc.
New York, N.Y., U.S.A.
But which page and which volume is what I sadly fail to remember.

Page 76 - Sandy, (1991) – *A Poem*
New York City
Mr. Ellsworth is our friend. He has been for a long time. He is famous for so many things, it would take books to describe any of them. His extraordinary garden in Connecticut, planted by himself, is one of those things. One early morning, when Spring was all around, it fell victim to the worst Ice Storm in fifty years. Sandy wrote him this poem in commiseration.

Page 77 - Snow Covered Landscape
Yuan Jiang, (1690-1730)
Chinese Painting
Ink and Colour on Silk
Courtesy of a Friend

Page 78-79 - Sun Tzü –*The Art of War*, pp.8-10
James Clavell, Editor, May, 1981
Hodder & Stoughton Publishers
London, England

Page 80 - Sandy, (1993) – *A Poem*
Exuma Cays
The Bahamas

WHY

He isn't going to die is he?

He is Cécile. He is.

He can't. He can't die. It isn't Time yet.

What do you think Cécile? You think Death just stands around waiting on Time?

The Doctors. The Doctors aren't working.

Right. It's been 5 1/2 weeks, 5 1/2 weeks of 105° temperature. 5 1/2 weeks of restless burning, turning – of Blood Poisoning in his shoulder, of rotten malevolent Coxycillin dripping agonizingly into his veins, and Nothing – Dead Flat Nothing Working. Nothing Curing Sandy. He's worse than ever. As for those doctors who let him totter out of bed so he could shake 400 hands at Convocation... Those doctors are crazy? They just cave in because Sandy gets to them the way he gets to everybody else? Even when he's dying? They cared? They didn't care. Nobody cares.

Mara cares.

Thank God for Mara – dropping everything. Arriving from Colorado in a raging blizzard to give her mother her first night off in Eternity.

Not Eternity Cécile. Why do you exaggerate everything?

Watching Sandy die <u>is</u> Eternity.

64 is too young to die.

The memories. The memories whirring around inside my head like a kaleidoscope. Sailing around the world on *Zolana*. **DIVING AT FUNAFUTI**, teaching his three little children – Mara 11, Fiona 9, Alastair 8 how to conserve the air in their tanks, how to make the air last, concentrating his years of deep sea exploring into Porpoise Training. Baby Porpoises. They looked so cunning with their periscopes, their tanks, their brightly coloured orange life vests playing Porpoise Games in the deep underwater clear – playing follow–their–leader–Daddy into canyons of incandescent coral.

JUMPING OUT OF AIRPLANES. The white rigidity of his face just before his first leap later transformed into exhilarated abandon as he took his wife dancing that same night – to celebrate – because he was still alive.

What about CF-POP, Alberta's first hot air balloon?

What about when he and Max Ward saw that high tension wire looming closer and closer until, in that laconic voice he always reserves for extreme danger: "Well Max, I guess we better jump." I guess they better had. Thirty feet below – onto grass. Not the way it happened with another comrade of Sandy's who, in the same week, crashed sixty feet below onto deadly concrete amidst the screams of horrified crowds.

No. Sandy was lucky.

It wasn't lucky when that huge ball of fire seared through those balloon cables. They could see it for miles. Everyone said.

It was lucky.

For three years **BEST IN THE WEST** racing Datsuns on weekends until finally coming third in the Canadian Nationals. Yes, I watched him once. Rolling over three times. He never spider webbed me into his audience again. Who wants to see their husband consumed by flames? All his life that Love Affair with Danger……

Best in the West. Engraved on all those pewter tankards he won for prizes. Over and over again. They're going to let Best in the West just plain die.

He always had time for everyone. Business everyone. Children everyone. You never have time for anyone. You're always running and running, trying to catch up. **YOU** never arrive. Each year **HE** arrives somewhere new.

Right.

Desolately I peered into the fire. 5:30 p.m.

Lots of people die.

NOT SANDY.

What if I made him something?

What can you make? You can't cook. You don't know how to sew. You don't paint. You can't knit. What **DO** you do anyway?

I write books.

Languishing unsubmitted for years. Trunkfuls of unsubmitted, unpublished manuscripts. Some writer. Anyway, who ever heard of anyone writing a book in one night? 5:30 p.m. You always go to bed at 10:00. You think people write books in four and one-half hours?

I could go to bed at 12:00. Just once.

Like a Hex? Like a Magic to ward off Evil?

Yes. If I did it myself, with my own hands.

But all you have is Scraps.

SCRAPS. That's it Cécile. All over the house, "Upstairs and Downstairs and in my Lady's Chamber". Hurry. Run. Everything Beautiful pasted behind all your Cupboard Doors. 35 years of Collecting from all over the world. All those Paintings and Textiles. Everything you both love.

What shall I call it?

A Scrapbook for Sandy. That's what to call it. That's a good name for a book Cécile. Hurry. Hurry and get started.

I hurried.

                 *   *   *

He didn't much care. The next morning when I gave it to him. This *Scrapbook for Sandy*. He was too sick. Only guess what? I read his chart. 104°. Not 105°. And then the next day 103°.

Do you think that was your book?

What do <u>you</u> think? He turned the corner didn't he – the very next morning when I gave him my book – after five and a half weeks? That's kind of funny, if you ask me.

Was it like all your Favourite Fairy Tales when you were a little girl in Inagua? The ones which began, "Once upon a time, a long time ago, there was a Princess . . . ?"

Yes. Hans Christian Anderson Fairy Tales about Ugly Toads turning into Enchanted Princes. A Magic Book for Sandy turning into a Talisman for Somebody Else.

Is that what you wish could happen?

That's what I wish.
Cécile E. Mactaggart
Scrapbook Editor
August 1, 1994

ALPHABETICAL INDEX
BY AUTHOR WHEREVER POSSIBLE
Page #

I trust that from this the reader may place more confidence in a work not carelessly undertaken, though produced in the spare time of other pursuits more closely followed. He should perhaps be told that it has occupied the leisure moments of not a few years; thus affording, often at long intervals, every opportunity for consideration and revision, and that in the score of care, at least, he has no need to mistrust it.

Dante Gabriel Rossetti
1828-1882
Exactly the opposite
for Scrapbooks